WITHDRAWN

JUST A MINUTE

BY BONNY BECKER

ILLUSTRATED BY JACK E. DAVIS

Simon & Schuster Books for Young Readers

NEW YORK LONDON TORONTO SYDNEY SINGAPORE

"Now, don't you move,"
said Johnny MacGuffin's mother.
"Stay right here while I shop.
Auntie Mabel will watch.
I'll be just a minute."

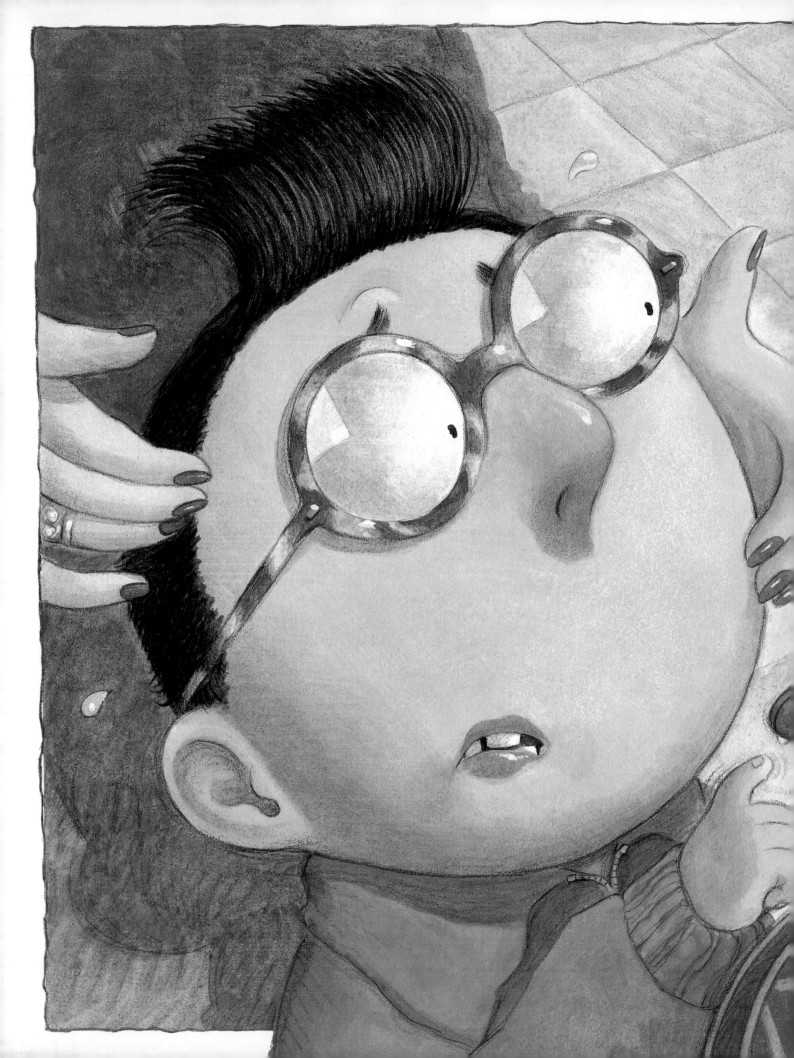

And she sailed away,
past the purses and plates,
up the up escalator
in Bindle's department store.
"But you'll take forever!" Johnny cried.
"When you get back I'll be fossilized."
But it was too late.
He was stuck in the basement of Bindle's again.

Stuck in the basement of Bindle's again,
he counted the squares of linoleum
all the way down to the newspaper stand. . . .
Thirty-one.
He counted the hairs on the third double chin
of Mabel buying socks. . . .
Four.
He counted the seconds on the clock.
One hundred and ten . . .
or was it minutes . . .
. . . or even hours?

It was Tuesday. Wasn't that true?
But calendar pages flew
like birds from their nest.
And church bells were tolling,
and shoppers were strolling
in their Sunday best.
Had a week gone by?
Or even more?

It was spring, not fall. He was really quite sure.
But outside the store,
leaves were blowing. . . .
Or, was it snowing?
And who was that fat man ho-ho-hoing?

It was Santa!

What was *he* doing here?

And those prancing, dancing plastic reindeer?

Had Mother been gone a whole year?

Where had she gotten to?

Suddenly he could feel hairs on his cheek!
His voice tumbled out in a squeak!
He was turning into a freak!

And it seemed to Johnny
he grew a foot or more,
got married, had five kids, and
bought a house on the hill,
waiting in Bindle's
department store.

Then his hair turned to gray
and all fell away.
And the clock on the wall stopped with rust.
The hill and his house crumbled to dust,
and beneath his feet, the floor
shifted with massive tectonic force.

Johnny thought Mother had better come soon,
as the sun shifted its course
and the seas rose and fell
and rose again.

But what could he do when the tides came in
and the sun burned to a cinder of vermilion . . .

but wait.

"Yoo-hoo, Johnny. Sorry I'm late."
Mother arrived with a brand-new dress,
new purple shoes, and a hat quite grand.
"Things took *just* a bit longer than planned."

On she marched through the double doors
of Bindle's eternal department store,
then turned and sighed, impatient,
as Johnny learned how to walk again.

"Now hurry up, dear.
We've miles more shopping
and miles more chores.

"Come along, now. Don't delay.
Goodness, Johnny, I haven't got all day!"

For Redd and Frank, with
love—B. B.
For Ralph Dovali—J. D.

SIMON & SCHUSTER BOOKS FOR YOUNG READERS

An imprint of Simon & Schuster Children's Publishing Division

1230 Avenue of the Americas, New York, New York 10020

Text copyright © 2003 by Bonny Becker

Illustrations copyright © 2003 by Jack E. Davis

All rights reserved, including the right of reproduction in whole or in part in any form.

SIMON & SCHUSTER BOOKS FOR YOUNG READERS is a trademark of Simon & Schuster.

Book design by Dan Potash

The text for this book was set in Wilke bold.

The illustrations are rendered in colored pencil, acrylic, dye and ink.

Manufactured in China

10 9 8 7 6 5 4 3 2 1

Library of Congress Cataloging-in-Publication Data

Becker, Bonny.

Just a minute / by Bonny Becker ; illustrated by Jack E. Davis.—1st ed.

p. cm.

Summary: While Johnny waits for his mother to finish her shopping, he feels that so much time has passed that he has become an old man.

ISBN 0-689-83374-1

[1. Time—Fiction.] I. Davis, Jack E. ill.

PZ7.B3814 Ju 2003

[E]—dc21   2001040093